Year Zero

PUBLISHING INFO

First Edition
Heartworm Press #93
Copyright @ Mark Lanegan and Wesley Eisold 2022
ISBN 979-8-9859385-0-0

All rights reserved. No part of this book may be reproduced or transmitted in any form or by any means whatsoever without express written permission from the author, except in the case of brief quotations embodied in critical articles and reviews. Please refer all pertinent questions to the publisher.

First published in the United States of America
   by Heartworm Press, Publishers
Book design by Studio Anthony Smyrski
Edited by Amy Lee
Printed in Canada by the Prolific Group
Photo by Shelley Brien

Mark Lanegan and Wesley Eisold

Year Zero

A World With No Flowers

TABLE OF CONTENTS

MARK LANEGAN

Sometimes It's Like	10
Toxic	11
Troika	13
To Miss CH	14
Year Zero	15
Futile Travelling	16
Look Out Joe!	18
These Vedic Cats	19
Walking To New Orleans	20
Twelve Hours Of Daybreak	22
People Are Always Dragging Me	23

The Great Michael Avedon	**24**
Animod	**25**
Salt In The Wound	**26**
Nightshade	**27**
Party Crasher	**28**
Shadow Dirge	**29**
Slow Turn	**30**
Run Of The Mill	**32**
Hey Terry Graham	**34**
C-4, C-5, C-6	**36**
Fragment For Jim Carroll	**39**
Head Injury 89	**40**

WESLEY EISOLD

Disclaimer #1	44
There Is A Cave At The Bottom of The Sea	45
Wild Flowers At Dusk	46
Dracula	47
I Haven't Come A Long Way	48
Cascade	53
We Want To Reissue Your Record	54
Anti Aging Cream	55
The Hole Of Bristol	56
Dandelion 2	57
A World With No Flowers	58

I Don't Know Why I Wrote This	59
Like Voodoo	60
Farewell Friend	61
Narcisa Redux	62
Slouching Towards Babylon	63
My Heart Broke So Easy	64
A Loaded Gun In The House Next Door	65
Vulture Hunter	66
23 Black Prayer Candles	67
Um Om	68
Baby I'm Blue	69
777 Evil	70

MARK LANEGAN

SOMETIMES IT'S LIKE

A mouthful of rain
Or a soundless scream
At times it's so good
You disappear
Fleeting, flickering
Sundown in stasis
Drastic colour wheel imaginings
Inverted horizons
Death's Head moths
Locusts
And plague
Seasons of despair
And dread
Dead men in uniform
Marching endlessly on parade

TOXIC

a chain drags a reliquary behind a Pontiac
throwing up sparks
I'm coming apart
at the shoulder
waiting for a different kind of ride
the solitary heathen gringo
writing on a wall
hummingbirds spit nectar
into my mouth
turning toxic
black letters hail down
like semi-automatic fire
filling the notebook
burning pages from an old testament
catching me off guard
and not while I'm ahead
sex theatre, semaphores
and grime
Hannibal's elephants
couldn't drag me over this mountain
I'm both boat and Fitzcarraldo now
bubbles of highway tar
shimmering beneath the tundra
say so, tell me off, shoot at my foot
making me slow dance
there's golden brown dirt
all over my face
staining the collar of my coat
with formaldehyde colour-wash

I'm unwelcome here, and rightly so
no rooster wants a wolf
in his henhouse
especially not a snake
dressed in wolf's clothing
I'm caught up in some metal teeth
both feet infected now
and no way out
of a house of mirrors
in collapse
sentencing a stranger
to life without parole
the car takes a left at the end of the street
and then bolts across the floodplains
the firmament rips open
heaven soaks my hair with a gallon of viscera
the hummingbird drowns in a rain barrel
I stand witness on the shoulder
having never, ever been here
at all

TROIKA

1. False flag

Summoned at seance
Unwanted parcel
    Arrival in post, blank page
Mundane set up
    And TB sheets

1. Sunspot for eyeball pendant

        Miles Davis vampires
    Pantomime stagecraft pull
        Punch and Judy strings with chastised
Satan in absentia

1. Elaborate con

There's more than one make believe
    Magician at work now
Someone else should have to die here
    A redder wolf should lose it's teeth

TO MISS CH

Zero false modesty
Ballsy, too
I was certainly put
In my place
Rather quickly

And there is something dangerously
Irresistible about your way
But I am sure you know that

My diseased mind, related to
A provider, that's what you do

As well as the heavy lifting
For lazy guys such as myself

This experience
Has felt like
Something that's happening again
A beautiful deja vu

I hope to live up
To the gloriously jaded
Expectations

Signed, ML

YEAR ZERO

This is year zero
And I am rootless again

Blissfully selfish

Too slothful, impatient, strung out, rude, someone said
        Evil
              What does that really
Mean anyway?

Apparently kindness is a requirement if one
Wishes to be human here
              Empathy, open heartedness and
Caring have never been a strong suit

I've heard it said that it's never too late to change
              But the damage has been done

      Year zero

I'm keeping a conflict journal
A list of my wrongdoings
So there won't be any disputes

And I can take my punishment
Like a man
        When I'm called out on the carpet

      In the registrars office

At hell

Mark Lanegan

FUTILE TRAVELLING

I think of R Lowell
Sitting at a desk writing like an apostle
Of himself
Electric liquid mercury razorblade
Visionary words

And his life studies
And his union dead

And his imitations
That drilled a hole
Straight through my head

I think of him in the psych ward
Speaking in tongues to the walls
And others

Lit up with a divine soul
Power that must
Have fucked those

Doctors sideways I think
Of him holding court
At a dinner party

And his criticism of
Writers and
Writing and poetry
And poets

He would have
Hated this, I know,
Immature, pointless
And amateur

And I think of him alone
On a plane flying from
Ireland to New York City

Holding the painting
Of his wife
Done by one of her previous
Husbands
In his hands

And I think of him
Dying in the back of a cab
From JFK
To nowhere

And how that doesn't
Seem fair but
Is maybe somehow fitting

LOOK OUT JOE!

Look out Joe!
I tried to warn you little brother
Listen to the words, man!
It's gonna burn you son
It's gonna bury you up!
Did you think I was talking to myself?
I've been dust for years now...

THESE VEDIC CATS

These Vedic cats
Coughing up fur balls
Of accurate informay

Stick in my craw, now
But I was the fool
Who went rummaging through their drawers

And saw what I shouldn't of
Now it's a one-way march
Straight to the death cot

WALKING TO NEW ORLEANS

smoke
ghost walking
sacred filament of
terrestrial empires fallen
marble streets and jazz funeral cortège

the rodents are burying a feral cat today
signifying victory I guess
and surrender

fermented kisses
vivid nightmares and peacetime casualties
the smell of humid decay
and magnolia blossoms
in the morning air

minor key melodies sung in
aboriginal dream sequence
making all the junkies cry
into their sleeves
until they get well and then it's
business as usual again

monuments, deities and hidden treasure
are all unknowns
to a louisiana armadillo
or swamp buck

I loved you and now you're gone

just like
all the rest

but I'll think of you the next time
I'm sitting alone
somewhere

and Fats
comes on the
radio

TWELVE HOURS OF DAYBREAK

L.A. to Tokyo
Breakfast and
Breakfast again
So many trips who can keep track?
Who would want to, really
That flight to Australia from Cali
Can be rough if it's turbulent the entire way
Have experienced that one multiple times
And Santiago to Auckland or Brisbane
A nail biter if you hit rain and wind
Because there's nothing below
Except endless expanse of wild deadly ocean
A jetliner couldn't land anywhere if it
Wanted to
Because such a runway doesn't exist out there
Buenos Aries to Paris another sleeper
You gotta sleep or else you can get caught up
In high anxiety
I took that ride the day after an Air France flight
Disappeared the night before
Flying roughly the same path
Only from Rio

It's a comfort when that happens

Because everyone knows
lightning rarely
Strikes twice

PEOPLE ARE ALWAYS DRAGGING ME

People are always dragging me
To a fucking graveyard
Paris, LA, Buenos Aries, Nola, Edinburgh, etc
You name it
I've likely been there
All those dead bodies
Either in the ground
Or in some dilapidated cement or metal box above
I'm not into it
Sure, I may have liked to
Have met some of these stiffs
Before they died
But not like this
What's the goddamn point?
They might as well put a urinal
At my grave
For all those guys who will line up
To piss on it

THE GREAT MICHAEL AVEDON

The great Michael Avedon
Gave me a call
My most excellent young brother
Wanting to take my portrait
For a collection with some very
Esteemed company
Flattering, of course
Except that I am an exceptionally
Unattractive person
Inside and out
And those with insight into
A person's soul
Or lack there of
Such as Michael,
Will surely capture that with
Their perceptive lense
And let the monster out of the bag
Who would then likely murder
An innocent child by the lake
And rampage through the village
Until it was burned to death in some barn
By the angry citizenry
It's just as well that I am stranded
In a foreign country, overstayed my legal
Welcome, head down, hiding out
And unable to leave for not being
Allowed to get back in
It's always the same story with guys like me
Always pulling some shady
Underhanded bullshit
Always driving sideways in reverse

ANIMOD

pleased
wrung out, bruised,
near annihilation
she's

punishment desired
sought to administer
too well, maybe
acted the part
i've

blindfold
gag
restraints
crop

instruments
modern servant trade

of a fractured soul
mirror

the scene
setting

SALT IN THE WOUND

Dance off to a standstill
/Holy/Holy/Holy/Fuk/
Someday ima soak
This land with blood

NIGHTSHADE

Stars hung like a casket

Spoken like a broken arm

So estranged from the world

Foreign body

Cinder block head

Glass jaw lemur eyes

Tattoos were birth marks

Covering other birth marks

Covering the mark

Still-born

Hey, strawberry where you going kid?

Downtown baby

To forget myself again

To the other end of the street

Where a man can be free

Mark Lanegan

PARTY CRASHER

Who invited you, tough guy?
Um...My buddy, Charlie, he's here somewhere
I've never heard of him and I live here...
Are you sure you guys are invited?
I guess one of your roommates knows him,
Anyway, I'll get out if you want me to lady
Jesus Christ, lady? Are you talking to my mom?
Sorry, it's just a figure of speech
Don't worry about it handsome
Can I get you another drink?
I'm ok with this one but
Can I ask you a sensitive question?
Does anyone here have any party favours?
I do but it'll cost you, she said
No worries I have plenty of cash, I said
I'm not selling for money, she said
Ah, ok, what's the deal then? I asked
Follow me, let's go to my bedroom, she said

Three hours later, my jaw cramped up like a pair of vice grips and pungent dried pussy juice all over my face and hair, I stumbled out with an eightball of the weakest cocaine ever

You gotta be careful of whose party
It is you're crashing

SHADOW DIRGE

Full on funeralesque
Funhouse
Turquoise rain
Dirtwater
Vipers nest
Two-bit hustler
Cheap fuck
Free in fact
His master's call
A tuneless bell
Bent at the spine
Struck with a skull
Translated to braille
Tire iron at the face
Long range sufferer
Stun gun
Bone collector
The trick to survival
Is take no prisoners
Everyone must pay
Everyone must hang
And every goddamn dog
Will have something to say
There's a girl from South Africa
Who's music I like
She messaged me today
It was an excellent surprise
Now I can die easy
At some future date
Yet to be decided

Mark Lanegan

SLOW TURN

This cold, white winter sun bores me to death
The blight beneath the green sprouts like
Immoral dandelions through the ice-works
And takes me down

Monstrous machinery of living

And is this really living?

Feeling the demoralizing drag of time now
And missing the constant rumble of travel
The blood of my torn existence
Thirty plus years always moving
And I don't want to stop now
I even miss the stage>
What's that about?
I've been handcuffed here
And yes, so has everyone else, but fuck that...
This is my mental health we're talking about!

Suddenly the trapdoor drops
Below me
A revenant laughs
And the wind plows through me

Twisting and turning
Bent backwards
And choking
Incessantly ringing the funeral bells

Death by hanging
Death by inertia...
And mindless aching emptiness
This is house arrest plain and simple
All that's missing is an ankle bracelet
And a visit from the P.O.
And all of Ireland has been sentenced, too
As has most of the world, everyone's dying

I would give anything to fly
To Miami for a weekend
And that's saying something

To be drifting in the blackness
Of the nighttime waves
Off the beach at Tel Aviv
In the warm Mediterranean
Under a dark wine red lunar eclipse
Just one more time...

RUN OF THE MILL

That was me you saw passed out, groveling
Head in hands, crying at the radio, pitiful
Carefully plotted suicidal ideation, shallow breathing,
Cracked out, cashed out, friendless,
Played out
Soot-stained windows
Fire escape a monument to fire itself
A shrine to my undoing
The glorious spectacle, come see!
Feet frozen
Ocular psychosis shame deception and all that jazz
Play it Satchmo, play it Bird, play it Trane
Until the birds have flown
Lay me down in a bed
Of white lilys cover my eyes so I don't see
This far flung crippling debacle
Take me back to Sicily
Send me to Bilbao
Athens
Melbourne
Mexico City
Manchester
Moscow
Istanbul
Brooklyn
Berlin
Copenhagen
Amsterdam
Chicago
Los Angeles

What's happened to all of my best haunts?
They've forgotten me there...
And come apart at the seams
This world has never had a place
For my kind and made that clear
Time and time thereafter
I got so run down you wouldn't believe it
Taxi, city bus, tractor and such
Optical illusions, auditory hallucinations
At 53rd and 3rd
Play it Dee Dee, play it Joey, play it Johnny
Until I leave the grave
Until I escape this heaven
Til my trial begins again
And I am able to plant my feet
Back on stony ground

HEY TERRY GRAHAM

Hey pal
Yeah it's me, Lanegan
The singer nobody has ever heard of
But apparently somebody had and told you about me
or you'd have not asked me to sing for you, right?
When it became clear I'd be unable to have even one
lousy rehearsal before playing someone else's entire
record in front of a live audience,
I was flattered to have been asked,
but I had to very humbly, very politely decline
And you could not resist downing me
In the L.A. Weekly for that, could you?
Because you are a rancid, flaming kennel of dogshit,
obviously.
So much for politeness then.
Since we have never met in person
I've had to wait awhile to say...Fuck.You.Terry.
And yeah, I'm a trillion miles away from being Lady
Gaga in terms of fame but then so are are you, in fact
probably a few trillion more from it, if I had to guess.
But I've always turned my back on that bullshit anyway,
everyone but you knows it's for the birds. With your
public insight into my dearth of popularity you revealed
what is paramount in your concerns, so it must be an
aching disappointment in your old age to be, well, let's
just say, a last place finisher in the relevance and vitality
sweepstakes. I can tell you from personal experience
that it doesn't matter how many boring, terribly written

books you crank out, nothing will ever change that. So kick rocks Terry, and do enjoy your sure to be continued spiralling obscurity little man. You were lucky enough to play drums with my genius friend for awhile but then I noticed you talked a mountain of trash about him too until someone must have clued you in to how history has rightly judged him to be a great and original artist. Something you have never been, nor will you ever be. There's some free immortality for you piss ant, you're welcome

C-4, C-5, C-6

Oh my motherfucking GOD!!
Pure agony...
Arm dead, a steady throb of excruciating pain
Between the shoulderblades
Emanating down my extremities
And up into the skull itself
No comfort whatsoever
Impatience level through the fucking ceiling

Newly clean, this posed a conundrum of sorts

A trip to the chiropractor in North Hollywood
Exacerbated things to the point of no return
It took a Sikh doctor in Beverly Hills
To sort out just how fucked it was
But laying on an ice pack round the clock
Had grown beyond tiresome
Even with the consistent blowjobs meant
To shut me up...give me some REAL relief!

Oxys were out of the question
The doc had been busted...

But hold on a second, what about the pharmacy?
Where I had an almost endless supply of
Scrips for yellow Norco?
Woodland Hills is a long ways from Altadena
Especially at rush hour but I was more than

Willing to do that drive for some strong-ish
Painkillers
Baby, I don't think this is a good idea! She said
Can't you hold on until the epidural next week?

I fucking promise you I will take as prescribed,
I promise! I'm not bullshitting you! This is
Critical!

Ok, but you have to let me give them
To you, all right?

Sure, baby whatever you say, just get me out
There before they close!

Later outside the pill mill where I had been way
Over-served forever, and where my signed record sat
Up on the wall I said: These guys are kinda sketchy
Sweetheart, wait here while I go get it
And handing over the bottle to my girlfriend
Back in the car, she gave me two and then
Dumped out the rest in her hand and counted
Them

What the fuck, why is there only fifty in here?
She asked, This label says sixty!
Fuck me! Those assholes shorted me eight? Again?
Goddamnit! I said

And then drifted off in that warm familiar glow
Ten yellow Norco dissolving in my stomach racing
Through my bloodstream to my brain

My neck still sore as hell
But my head a million times better

FRAGMENT FOR JIM CARROLL

I'm sure you wanted to live more than die
And although I never knew you
I've been some places you've been
I was sorry to hear you'd gone so soon
But I admire that huge willingness of spirit
And dogged determination to write
One more song
One more poem
And to keep standing
In a lightning storm
To conjure fire
Even when it's the very last thing
You're ever gonna do

Mark Lanegan

HEAD INJURY 89

I drifted in a stupor, dreaming
Backwards up the down escalator
Swimming amongst the frostbitten treetops
For years on end
Bleeding reptile tears
From tar filled
Knife wound contusions
No EMT could stitch up
Stiff stoicism
A Baalbek megalith
I came untethered
And slid off the barge in a maelstrom
Pummeled by waves
Skyscraper high
Sunk miles to the floor of the Marianas Trench
Forehead inches above a shelf
White flag in mouth
Target practice for haggard troops
Stuffed animals, erasers and shot-glasses
Conduits of nothingness
Stolen magic, more storms, unknown histories
American primitivism
Stoked on his own fires, choked out on his own ashes
A Phoenix flattened
Lazarus reburied
Rough alchemy
Strange visions, wooden horses and perversion
Cronos takes the train through
Peruvian mudslides, rotting infrastructure,
Wings peppered with buckshot, captain grounded,

Charged treason
Court martial, trial and death sentence
DNA disordered, puzzles jigsawed
Fragments, comedy, whirlpools of disgust
Salt lick, green apples, cumstains and brick
Trash vortex, Bermuda bungalow
Mercenary, cut-throat
Planetary provision
A dog evolves in reverse
Bares his teeth and whines underwater
Earthquake activity secret society
Civilisation retracted
Genetic alteration, Paper tiger, criminal conspiracies
Gnostic, pagan, paternalist journalists
Mathematics of necessity
Cataclysm, floods
Industry in division
The Mastodon domesticated, jail cell, cigarette,
Derelict tollbooth
Heartsick, dopesick, negative sophistication
Beauty ethereal bought and sold
Weeds grown through the wallpaper
A cloud of butterflies released
Monarchs abdicated
An animal put down
Time runs past tense
The dreamer in surrender
Re-holsters his pistols
And finally shoots for sleep

WESLEY EISOLD

DISCLAIMER #1

I should have made my first poem
In the second book with Mark better.
There are so many reasons why I didn't do that.
I tried so hard and tried it all...
From tylenol to tramadol to trileptal
Xanax and topamax
With more rings and a nicer suit
Ashwagandha and dragon fruit
Just driving with drivel until the wheels wear out
At the end of the road with no tracks to bury
Pollen
Penicillin
Imperialism
Impotence
There are so many reasons why I didn't do that..
But here it is, the first poem
In the second book with Mark.
A poem that should have been better.

THERE IS A CAVE AT THE BOTTOM OF THE SEA

I did not die
Or fall on Jesus
By the time the flood arrived
I just sank with the weight
Of the rock in my heart

> Titanic
> Krakatoa
> Genesta
> Woolf

I did descend
As stubborn as me
In a cave so deep
At the bottom of the sea

Wesley Eisold

WILD FLOWERS AT DUSK

It's easy to see all that's wrong in the garden
The ivy covered in dust
The gardenia that never grows
The spider plants strangled in web
And the slow leak of the fountain
Against my will to refill

You know the flowers will die
But plant them anyway
It's all of these little resurrections that
Keep us rising from the dirt

DRACULA

Your poem sucks
Here
Have this
One

I HAVEN'T COME A LONG WAY

Plymouth rock sinks in the sand
As freedom's last firework flickers
Like a lighter you found in your pocket
That you don't know how you got

America was seasonal
And I sat on a broken tractor
In an abandoned barn
In the middle of 200
Neglected corn fields
That once seemed to grow on
Towards forever
Even though they had died
Some twenty years before

Staring out across the
The golden stalks of
Pennsylvania wildlife
Disintegration brown
Fading deer
Falling geese
I could feel an emptiness
In my pit that outgrew Carlisle
But good enough
To remember
Like the present
As a memory
You're reminiscing of
Even as you're living it
           Down

And with my bored wandering blood
Made of
    Massachusetts
    North Carolina
    By way of
    Germany
    And
    Scotland

I stole a cigarette
From my Grandmother's jacket
And burnt a hole in the skin
Above my right hip
To see what feeling
Might feel like

The Soviet occupation of Hungary
Left in 1991
The same year I arrived
With my bored wandering blood
Greeted by military escort
And shortly after some hash
Along the Serbian border
They danced and drank
And me so neglected
I dreamt of being molested
But failed at that
So scoured the Unicum sips
Until sleep put me at ease

From a Florida dirt hill
Buried 80's porno
Under a rock
Behind weeds
Stashed by the neighbor
Who waved his shotgun at me and
Who tried burning his house down
After his sister and her friends
Denied his advances
Matthew was his name
Sent from a military base
To a military school
Escorted by police
From his General father's shame
And his mother's Mary Kay tears
As his sister continued to
Cheer for the local team
Last time I was in Jacksonville
They gave me a green room
That was just the outside back of the bar
With rock and weeds and
Blurred sex drawings
Above teenagers with awkward skin
Smoking no name cigarettes
On their asses against the wall
On their break from the sandwich shop
No one's gone in all day
On the wall above them
I read a message
"ACAB DIE"
Step on the smoke

I haven't come a long way
Alcohol is still open and
These are the drinks
They've driven us to
Kool aid stained lips
Around a mouth that
Can't find the words
On my face that
Can't hide the
> Fear
> Love
> Depression
> Progression
> Dementia

The car dealerships are still open and
These are the brinks
They've driven you to
Down the yellow brick road
All lined with roadside flowers
> Homelessness
> Prostitution
> Cancer
> Addiction
> Religion

California is burning...
Throw me in the forest fire

See how easy it can all be
To take everything that gives you hope

Wesley Eisold

Beware of those saying
  "Pollution is on the decline"
These are just people
Who've never noticed the sky
They've gone from worshipping
To playing God
  Your cash
  Your love
  Your spirit
  Your home
  Your family

And I look back over the eroding coasts
Recalling all that I've found
And all that I've lost
  Forsaken
  Forgotten
  Forever
  Foreboding

How the youth you don't miss
Sheds inside you still
Skin turning inside out
So that all you see
Is the journey
And all the long ways
I have come
And how lovely it has been
To grow away from it all
To outlive the stalks
To arrive here
On this day
With you

CASCADE

It's never just peace
You know,
The bridge burns from both ends

About all that rain coming down -
It's not heroic
       just wet
       and distracting
       and
Now you know why I spent so many years indoors
Wrapped in her arms

The dream was to outrun the avalanche
To enjoy the meadow at ease
Before the sun went out
Before the tar blackened
The sanctuary

Like the swallow
I have fought for love
Flown high and gone low
For and against nature
Through storm and sea
But always returned
To the nest of your love

WE WANT TO REISSUE YOUR RECORD

Think of me as a 1990
Eight hole doc marten
Kicking your teeth in
Across the highway

ANTI AGING CREAM

Learning is the least attractive
      Part of life
You were all so beautiful
When you knew nothing

THE HOLE OF BRISTOL

In my chest an endless wish
  well you know where to rest your anchor
Going down on you for escapism
  I thought we'd both get off this bad trip
My subscription was addiction to long walks
Solemn cigarettes too early or late
  In a strange state colored New England
My love is infinite, finite and
Definitely defined

DANDELION 2

I swayed for as long as I could
Through each type of season
I was hot then wet then dry again

But ultimately my head was blown to the wind

A WORLD WITH NO FLOWERS

Leave the garden gate open
Too long and
The devil will come in

Then you will only grow
A world with no flowers

Love can't keep living off
This dirty soil
Without conviction
We will wilt

There is no beauty
In the corroded weeded soul
Of the savage
Just ruins of the palace
Where once bloomed an empire

I have locked the garden gate
Just now
The devil is frustrated

But I don't want to live in
A world with no flowers

I DON'T KNOW WHY
I WROTE THIS

Somehow my cock
Never stopped growing
Even tho
Life is a series
Of sanctions
To the will
And
Everything I see
Turns me off

LIKE VOODOO

That was the sound of Catholicism falling
Into the dark corners of the world
Forgotten except by little votives
Glowing slow
In the dark corners of the world
Palm reading spells
Tie dyed monastery
Hail Mary
Chanted underground
Aching inside my heart
In the dark corners of the world
Creaks
Desperation bones
Over the hardwood floors
Jesus Christ
Gris Gris
Sterilization
DNA
Baby Bats
Concertina Wire
Super Flower
Blood Moon
Dymphna Daze
Lucadia and I
Took a walk in the woods
And never came back

FAREWELL FRIEND

Swim with me in the poison sea
Make a wish on ballistic shooting stars
Waste your freedom in the virtual
Typical Hypocritical Heroic Vitriol
Fantasy is reality

We could talk about the road
But it's just a means made by other men
So many paved
So few drivers
I pray I'll see the irreplaceable again
On the astral plane
Where no passenger
Sans vision
Can navigate

I will take the Lord's reigns
Steer my way to you
Wherever you are
Whatever you become

Wesley Eisold

NARCISA REDUX

On take away from this is
a bunch of narcissists
read books on narcissism
and now think they are experts

SLOUCHING TOWARDS BABYLON

Sabotage meets me
At the door of my dreams
Holding Voltaire's Book Of Fate
In its calm crippled hug
And I'm spiraling
Like water
Drunk on itself
Yet still dehydrated
Despite this
All consuming
Instinct

The problem is
I am trying to overcome
Myself...

I cannot love
The one I love

You come in
Like the Saint of Everything
    Etna
    Expedite
    Eternal
    Etcetera

My admission was to drown in the waves
Beneath the drink and over it all
My intercession was to swim in your love
Above the surface and under God

Wesley Eisold

MY HEART BROKE SO EASY

It was nothing,
Like buying cigarettes
With a fake ID
At midnight
In nowhere America

A LOADED GUN IN THE HOUSE NEXT DOOR

They're not taking all the books into the digital sphere
Once they burn them all there'll be no proof of them
Henry Miller library erodes into the sea
Bukowski's race track demolished by horses
Whitman and Ginsberg burning in hell
And the bible bursts into a small puff of smoke
Bury the ashes
Grow Utopia
      Feel Nothing
      Know Nothing
      Love Nothing

Wesley Eisold

VULTURE HUNTER

You pick at death
Like your life depends on it

I've had you in my sights
Since the beginning of the end

23 BLACK PRAYER CANDLES

23 black prayer candles
Burning in a broken fireplace
I knew this affair with darkness
Could not last forever
But loved having
Your fire in my corner

UM OM

Lanegan suggested meditation
He says,
You just think of
A positive thought
And repeat it

I said,
How do you think of
A positive thought?

BABY I'M BLUE

I could have loved you
In another life
If my carcass
Was made of
Blue agave
Instead of
White light

Wesley Eisold

777 EVIL

All hail the King of the Underworld
Who reigns upon
    cowards
    posers
    phony rock and rollers
With abscess and access
Comas and heart attacks
Sex swings and handguns
The golden voice with the golden smile
From here and there
And a little bit of everywhere

Deep in the bible black heart of resistance
Towering over Los Angeles beyond with
    peach red bull
    camel crush
    and tamarind candies
Stoned in the teenage winter
Faced down in the field
Freedom rings in and out of hell
And always answer my calls

You say,
It feels like I died
A horrible painful death
Lasting years
And no one noticed

Listen Old Scratch,
Everyone noticed
They always do
It's just their frustration
That kept them so quiet

Tucked away from the streets
They made their beds
In safe houses
All across your empire

Dead but living
Vs.
Alive but dead

We laughed
Just knowing that
We could burn
The whole world
If we wanted to

They say,
Live by the sword
Die by the sword
You did not suffer
But beheaded
So many fools

Wesley Eisold

God paints a portrait
As the devil of heaven
Smiling with horns
And cool in the flames
Wearing a cross for a compass
And the cosmos for rings
It's a strange religion
Where even death
Cannot outlive
The King

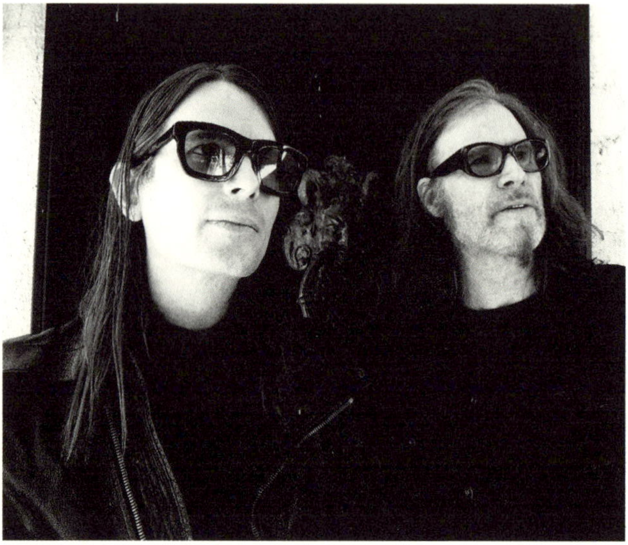